In Memory of Marisa Higgins

For Sylvie, the Higgins family, the Crosbie family,

my family, and all those we've lost too soon.

–J.R.

The Memory Box

A Book About Grief

By Joanna Rowland

Illustrations by Thea Baker

I lost my balloon once.
I tried so hard to hold on tight,
to never let it go.

But it was windy and I was running.

I watched it fly
higher than the trees, above the
clouds, past where I couldn't see.
I was sad.

But not as sad as I am now.
I can always get another balloon.
But I can never have another you.
I miss you.

Sometimes, I wonder what
happens to your love
now that you're gone?
Did it die too?

Because I'm scared
I'll forget you.

Sometimes, I wish I could
still give you a hug.
I would hug you so tight
in a great big bear hug
and never let go.

I'm making a
box so I won't
forget you,

with our memories like sand from the beach
where we played and left footprints as we
ran from crashing waves.

I want to
go everywhere
we've been,

everywhere
you've been,

everywhere we wanted to go.

I go to places that help me think of you.

I look around and remember.
It makes me smile.
Then I find the perfect thing
for my memory box.

MEMORY

Some days are good. I laugh. I smile.

Other days, I wonder if I'll ever
stop feeling sad you're gone.

But I always think of you.
So many things remind me of you.

Today I'm asking everyone about their
favorite memories of you.
Silly. Sweet. Some, just so *you*.
I'm listening to every word,
imagining you laughing with us.

It helps me when I think
about our special times.
And it even helps to still do the things
we'd planned to do together.

You're still with me
in my heart.

Now I'm making new memories.
My first time on a roller coaster,

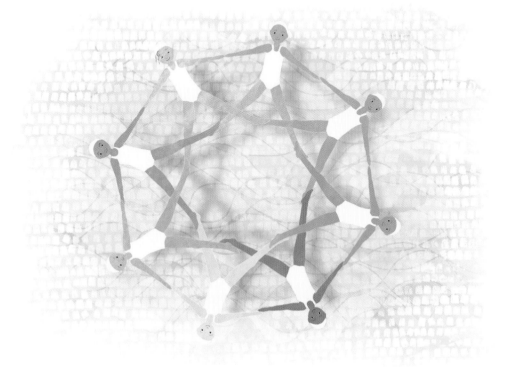

trying a new sport,

exploring a new place.

I'll always share these
memories with you.

I was afraid I would forget you.
But I won't.

You'll always be with me
no matter where I go.
Whenever I miss you
I'll think of you.

And I'll never forget.

Helping Children Process Grief

By Mary Lindberg

The Memory Box explores two questions that help
us understand how children deal with grief:

Will I forget my loved one?

When kids experience the death of a loved one, everyday routines, old assumptions, and expectations for the future are suddenly upended. One of the most profound changes kids face is the loss of their old identity. When kids worry that they will forget a person, they are also worrying that they will forget who they were with that person. Mr. Rogers, the beloved children's television host, reminded us that when tragedy strikes for kids, the first thing they want to know is, "How will this affect me?" In Rowland's book, after the young girl processes her grief, she feels reassured that she won't forget. In other words, she'll be okay. That's an enormous comfort for children. One way to help children move through their grief is to talk normally with them about their loved one. Talking about grief can be hard, but please don't be afraid to try. Grief becomes so much more complicated when it's considered a forbidden topic.

What do I do with my feelings?

The girl in *The Memory Box* feels sadness, fear, wonder, loneliness, and reassurance as she walks through her loss. That's very normal! Younger children might not have the words to express what they are going through, so they displace their feelings of grief into ongoing frustration and anger. Younger kids tend to be more literal and practical, anxious to figure out what happens next. Older kids are able to articulate their feelings better, but may be more susceptible to other feelings related to loss, like fear of losing other loved ones, concern about money, or guilt about getting on with one's life. Young or old, grief presents a struggle for all of us – both kids and adults! We have to simultaneously let go and hold on to someone we loved. It's important to stay in close touch with kids who are grieving, because they are going back and forth between these two realities– letting go and holding on.

If you know a child who is dealing with loss, here are some ways you can help them process their grief:

- Like the girl in this book, start a box of memories of a lost loved one. A memory box will help children overcome the fear that they will forget their loved one, and give them a physical activity to symbolically process their complicated emotions.

- Find support groups for families and kids. It helps kids tremendously to know that others share their experience!

- If you are religious, ask a leader from your faith tradition to meet with you and the child to talk about your faith's beliefs about life and death.

- On the anniversary of your loved one's death, share your memories with family, friends, or another community you treasure. Bake a favorite treat that your loved one appreciated and share music and pictures.

&

Mary Lindberg holds a Master of Divinity degree from Pacific Lutheran Theological Seminary in Berkeley, California. She has worked with children and families experiencing grief and loss as a hospital chaplain at Lutheran General Hospital and Seattle Cancer Care Alliance.

Thanks to Jessica Taylor for reading every version of this book, and to my editor Andrew DeYoung and illustrator Thea Baker for bringing my words to life in the most beautiful way. I can never thank you enough.

– J.R.

First edition published 2017
Printed in the USA
23 22 21 20 19 18 17   1 2 3 4 5 6 7 8

ISBN: 978-1-5064-2672-3

Book design by: Sarah DeYoung/Mighty Media

Library of Congress Cataloging-in-Publication Data

Names: Rowland, Joanna, author. | Baker, Thea, illustrator.
Title: The memory box : a book about grief / by Joanna Rowland ; illustrated
  by Thea Baker.
Description: First edition. | Minneapolis : Sparkhouse Family, 2017. |
  Summary: Grieving over the death of a special person, a young child
  creates a memory box to keep mementos and written memories of the loved
  one. Includes a guide for parents with information from a Christian
  perspective on helping manage the complex and difficult emotions children
  feel when they lose someone they love, as well as suggestions on how to
  create their own memory box.
Identifiers: LCCN 2017013488 | ISBN 9781506426723 (alk. paper)
Subjects: | CYAC: Grief--Fiction. | Death--Fiction. | Christian life--Fiction.
Classification: LCC PZ7.R7972 Me 2017 | DDC [E]--dc23
LC record available at https://lccn.loc.gov/2017013488

VN0004589; 9781506426723; JUN2017

Sparkhouse Family
510 Marquette Avenue
Minneapolis, MN 55402
sparkhouse.org

Joanna Rowland grew up in Sacramento, California, where she still lives today with her husband and three children. She teaches kindergarten by day and writes picture books at night. In the summer you'll find her at the pool coaching synchronized swimming or cozying up with a book.

Thea Baker grew up in a country town in England. She is currently living in Australia and working internationally as a children's illustrator. Thea obtained her BA (Hons) Degree in illustration at the prestigious Falmouth University. Her dissertation was on the subject of grief in children's books.